THE RUGRATS' JOKE BOOK

ha ha ha ha ha ha ha ha ha ha ha ha ha ha

Based on the TV series *Rugrats*® created by Klasky/Csupo Inc. and Paul Germain
as seen on Nickelodeon®

SIMON SPOTLIGHT
An imprint of Simon & Schuster Children's Publishing Division
1230 Avenue of the Americas, New York, New York 10020

SIMON SPOTLIGHT and colophon are registered trademarks
of Simon & Schuster.

Manufactured in the United States of America

First Edition   10 9 8 7 6 5 4 3 2 1

ISBN 0-689-82037-2

THE RUGRATS' JOKE BOOK

BY DAVID LEWMAN

Simon Spotlight/Nickelodeon

How are Rugrats like ink?
They're kept in a pen.

Knock, knock.
Who's there?
Tommy.
Tommy who?
Tommy the truth—why's this door locked?

Knock, knock.
Who's there?
Woodchuck.
Woodchuck who?
Would Chuckie like to come out and play?

If Tommy's cousin were a sandwich, what kind would she be?
Peanut butter Angelica.

If Angelica lived in the ocean, what would she be?
A sel-fish.

Why did Angelica dump beetles and worms on Tommy?
She wanted to make a baby buggy.

Where does Lil's twin go when he's out of gas?
The Philling station.

What do you call Lil's twin after he plays in the mud?
Philthy.

Is Phil's twin big?
No, she's Lil.

Knock, knock.
Who's there?
Didi.
Didi who?
Did he or didn't he lock this door?

Knock, knock.
Who's there?
Stu.
Stu who?
'S too cold out—let me in.

Why did Stu imitate his wife?
He wanted to do a good Didi.

What do you get if you cross Tommy's dad with a cow?
Beef Stu.

Who is Phil & Lil's favorite Wizard of Oz character?
The Twin Man.

How can you tell when Angelica's on the phone?
You get a bossy signal.

How is Angelica like a banana?
They both spoil easily.

Knock, knock.
Who's there?
Drool.
Drool who?
**Drew'll be here soon
to pick up Angelica.**

Why does Chuckie think his teeth cost two dollars?
Angelica says he has two buck teeth.

If the Finster baby were a bath toy, what kind would he be?
A rubber Chuckie.

Why is Chuckie afraid of his stroller?
Because every sTROLLer has a TROLL in it.

Why did Chuckie crawl in the fireplace?
He wanted to put on a new soot.

What has white fur, big claws, and wheels?
A stroller bear.

What do baby cats wear?
Diapurrs.

What do you get if you cross a teething ring with a chicken?
A pacifryer.

What do fish use to calm their babies?
A bassifier.

Why did Reptar get a ticket?
He ran through a stomp sign.

What's big and scary and lives in the toaster?
A Reptart.

What happened to the toaster when Tommy put jelly in it?
It jammed.

What's cute and fuzzy and lives at the North Pole?
A teddy brrr.

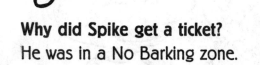

Why did Spike get a ticket?
He was in a No Barking zone.

What's the only kind of bone Spike won't eat?
A trombone.

What kind of dog is best with babies?
A Baby Setter.

Which farm animal is best with babies?
A nanny goat.

What kind of keys does Tommy like to carry?
Cookies.

Why did Chuckie drool on his fruit?
He wanted a banana spit.

What did Didi say when she saw Chuckie's shirt?
"There's been a slobbery!"

Why should Chuckie play basketball someday?
Because he's already a great dribbler.

What do you get when you cross a canary with a horse?
A tweeter-trotter.

**What do you get when you
cross an alligator and a vegetable?**
Croccoli.

**What do you get when you cross a dinosaur
and a vegetable?**
A broccosaurus.

Why did Tommy pull the plug in the bathtub?
He wanted to go for a drain ride.

Why did the bubble leave the bath?
He was looking for his pop.

When is a duck not a duck?
When he's afloat.

What do you get when you take a bath in chocolate?
Milk suds.

25

If Phil and Lil were a piece of fruit, what kind would they be?
A pear.

How do you make an orange go faster?
Give it more juice.

What's crunchy, tasty, and very dirty?
A grime cracker.

What did the pork chop say to the steak?
"Nice to meat you."

What does a cat call a boo-boo?
A meowie.

What does Spike call a boo-boo?
A bow-wowie.

Knock, knock.
Who's there?
Pea cub.
Pea cub who?
I see you!

What did Phil say when he saw Lil's tangled shoelaces?
"Did knot!"

What did Lil say when she saw Phil's missing button?
"Did sew!"

Why did Tommy wave at his seat?
It was a hi chair.

What do mommy ghosts sing to their baby ghosts?
Lullaboos.

What did the mommy needle say to the baby needle?
"It's way past your threadtime."

Why did Angelica ask to visit the mall?
She wanted to go buy-buy.

What does Angelica think the magic words are?
"Tease" and "prank you."

How does Angelica ask for a tissue?
"Pretty sneeze with booger on top?"

**Why did Tommy leave his crib
after dark?**
He wanted to be a night crawler.

**What do you call a baby's sock full of ice
cream?**
A tutti-frutti bootie.

Where did Chuckie learn all about ice cream?
In sundae school.

Why did Tommy pretend to cry?
He wanted to play bawl.

Knock, knock.
Who's there?
Kanger.
Kanger who?
No, but I do have a pocket.

Knock, knock.
Who's there?
Clark O'Doodle.
Clark O'Doodle who?
I didn't know you were a rooster.

What's warm, tasty, and very clean?
Chicken noodle soap.

Knock, knock.
Who's there?
Kook.
Kook who?
Yes, you certainly are.

Knock, knock.
Who's there?
Want.
Want who?
Very good! Now try counting to three!

If Cynthia were a dog, what kind would she be?
A dollmation.

Knock, knock.
Who's there?
Snap.
Snap who?
'S nap time—go to sleep.

What's the difference between a kid on Halloween and Angelica every day?
One likes to trick-or-treat, and the other thinks it's a treat to trick.

Where does Angelica get ideas for new pranks?
In the tricktionary.

What are Angelica's best preschool subjects?
Greeding, griping, and arithmetrick.

Is it true that Tommy isn't really bald?
No, that's just hairsay.

What kind of storm did Chuckie get caught in?
A worrycane.

Why did Tommy put pennies in his diaper?
It needed to be changed.
Did it work?
No, it still had a bad cent.

Will Tommy have fun learning to use the toilet?
Yes, he'll be the life of the potty.

What would you call Spike if he wore a mask and rode a horse?
The Bone Ranger.

Where can you find more information about Tommy's dog?
The Enspikelopedia.

Where do the Pickles leave Spike when they go shopping?
In the barking lot.

Why did Tommy crawl under Spike?
He wanted a woof over his head.

Why did Spike get thrown out of the choir?
He kept singing arf-key.

What did the mongoose have on her birthday?
Snake and ice cream.

Which is braver—a stone or a stump?
A stone, because it's a little boulder.

What game do babies play wearing diapers?
Hide & Leak.

Knock, knock.
Who's there?
Phillip.
Phillip who?
Fill up my bottle—I'm starving!

What do you call a bunch of smelly stars?
The Big Diaper.

What's the babies' motto?
"If at first you don't succeed, cry, cry again."